Letterland

Let's All Go to the Seaside

by Domenica Maxted

Illustrated by the Geri Livingston Studio

The Characters

Kicking King

Quarrelsome
Queen

Noisy Nick

Sammy
Snake

Uppy
Umbrella

Plus: Narrator **and** Chorus Leader

Let's All Go to the Seaside

Narrator

In Letterland, one summer's day,
everyone's off to the beach to play.
Quarrelsome Queen, bucket in hand,
prepares for playing in the sand.

Quarrelsome Queen

Now, have I got everything?
bucket
spade
sun hat
swimming costume

[Holds up objects as she names them.]

Narrator

Let us help the busy queen and
say the things that we have seen.

Chorus

    bucket

    spade

    sun hat

    swimming costume

[*Kicking King comes in with kite.*]

Kicking King

    Don't forget the kite!

Quarrelsome Queen

Kite! Why should I need a kite?

Kicking King

For flying in the sky and having fun, of course.

Quarrelsome Queen
Oh, very well. Let's try again.

Quarrelsome Queen and Chorus
bucket
spade
sun hat
swimming costume
kite

Kicking King
Are you ready? Let's go!

[*Sammy Snake comes in with sun block.*]

Sammy Snake

Oh, Quarrelsome Queen! You've forgotten something really important.

Quarrelsome Queen

What is it, Sammy? I'm in a hurry.

Sammy Snake

Sun block.

Quarrelsome Queen

Oh, that *is* important. You should always put on sun block if you are going to be in the sun.

Narrator

Sammy's right, that much is plain. So we must say the list again.

Chorus

bucket
spade
sun hat
swimming costume
kite
sun block

Quarrelsome Queen

Now, let's go!

[*Noisy Nick comes in with a net.*]

Noisy Nick

Oh, Quarrelsome Queen! You've forgotten something.

Quarrelsome Queen

What is it, Noisy Nick? I don't want anything noisy, thank you very much.

Noisy Nick

What about a net so you can catch fish?

Quarrelsome Queen

That is quite a good idea, Noisy Nick.

Kicking King

Quick, let's pack the net and go.

Narrator

Before we head off for the shore,
let us say the list once more.

Chorus
> bucket
> spade
> sun hat
> swimming costume
> kite
> sun block
> net

Quarrelsome Queen
> Come on! Let's go!

Narrator
> Quarrelsome Queen, please don't
>   go yet.
> You've forgotten something else,
>   I bet.

Quarrelsome Queen
> What?

Narrator
> What's the thing you should
> have with you,
> wherever you are or
> whatever you do?

Chorus
> Umbrella!

Quarrelsome Queen
> Oh, no! I've forgotten my
> umbrella! I must have my
> umbrella!

[*Uppy Umbrella comes in holding her umbrella.*]

Uppy Umbrella

Did someone say "my umbrella"?

Quarrelsome Queen

Oh, Uppy! You've remembered my umbrella! Thank you so much!

Uppy Umbrella

It's my pleasure, my Queen. Now let's make a word before we go!

[Sammy Snake, Uppy Umbrella and Noisy Nick stand together to form the word 'sun'.]

Chorus
    Sun!

Narrator

Narrator

Off they go to have some fun,
to swim and play in the summer sun.
And, just like them, we too must learn
to wear sun block, or we may burn.

Tips for Teachers

This play can be used for a performance (in class or assembly), for group reading, or as part of your daily phonics teaching.

The play has six spoken parts, including the Narrator who can either be yourself or an older child. The other five parts are played by children – it doesn't matter if the characters are played by boys or girls. A sixth child can act as Chorus Leader, in charge of holding up the chorus cards (see opposite). This role provides a good opportunity for a less able reader to become fully involved in the activities. The Chorus consists of the rest of the class or the audience; alternatively, it could be spoken just by the characters in the play.

Let's All Go to the Seaside is especially written to provide practice in literacy skills, including initial sounds, rhyming words, alliteration and word building. Reading or performing this play in groups helps improve speaking and listening skills as well as encouraging social and personal development.

Preparation

Before starting work on the play:

- Explain to the children how stories may be told in various ways, and that a 'play' allows them to pretend they're people in a story. Discuss how actors on TV and in films have to learn their words and rehearse their roles, as if acting in a play.

- Tell the children at the outset if the play is to be performed for an audience. If it is, this will help motivate everyone to re-read their parts until they have achieved real fluency and lively expression.

- Briefly, in your own words, tell the story of the play.

- Explain the special words used in relation to the play, for example, 'narrator', 'chorus', 'props'.

- Encourage the children to use plenty of expression when reading their parts.

- Write the chorus parts in large print on a series of cards, or a flipchart – your class may enjoy doing this themselves.

Props and costumes

Let's All Go to the Seaside uses the following props: bucket, spade, sun hat, swimming costume, kite, bottle or tube of sun block, and fishing net. The children could bring these in as part of a topic on the seaside or, alternatively, they could just use pictures of the objects instead.

All the characters should have their letters, in lower case, on their chests or on headbands to help identify themselves to the audience. This will also allow them to form the 'live spelling' word at the end of the play. The *Letterland Big Picture Code Cards* are useful for this purpose because they will show up well at a distance.

In addition, the characters could also wear or carry the following costumes and props to help represent their Letterland characters:

Quarrelsome Queen: crown
Kicking King: crown, football boots
Sammy Snake: headband with card or felt snake's head
Noisy Nick: drum or other noisy instrument
Uppy Umbrella: umbrella

Cross-curricular links

Let's All Go to the Seaside provides plenty of opportunities for cross-curricular links, for example:

Literacy: play *Kim's Game* – "I went to the seaside and I took…"; make lists of what to take for a day at the seaside; find and read poems about the sun, the sea or kites.

Science: discuss the importance of sun safety.

D&T: Design and make kites, use art package (IT), write instructions (Literacy).

PSE: discuss safety on the beach; stranger danger; litter; the importance of knowing your name and address.

Letterland

Learning with Letterland

Log on to the full range of Letterland titles at
www.letterland.com